THE VOYAGES OF
ODYSSEUS

HOMER

THE VOYAGES OF ODYSSEUS

TRANSLATED BY E. V. RIEU

Revised translation by D.C.H. Rieu
in consultation with Peter V. Jones

PENGUIN BOOKS

PENGUIN BOOKS
Published by the Penguin Group
Penguin Books USA Inc., 375 Hudson Street,
New York, New York 10014, U.S.A.
Penguin Books Ltd, 27 Wrights Lane,
London W8 5TZ, England
Penguin Books Australia Ltd, Ringwood,
Victoria, Australia
Penguin Books Canada Ltd, 10 Alcorn Avenue,
Toronto, Ontario, Canada M4V 3B2
Penguin Books (N.Z.) Ltd, 182–190 Wairau Road,
Auckland 10, New Zealand

Penguin Books Ltd, Registered Offices:
Harmondsworth, Middlesex, England

Published in Penguin Books 1995

Translation copyright E. V. Rieu, 1946
Revised translation copyright © the Estate of the late E. V. Rieu
and D. C. H. Rieu, 1991
All rights reserved

These extracts are from E. V. Rieu's translation of *The Odyssey*
by Homer, published by Penguin Books.

ISBN 0 14 60.0151 6

Printed in the United States of America

CONTENTS

The Cyclops

In answer to the King, this is how Odysseus, the man of many resources, began his tale:

'King Alcinous, most illustrious of all your people, it is indeed a lovely thing to hear a bard such as this, with a voice like the voice of the gods. I myself feel that there is nothing more delightful than when the festive mood reigns in the hearts of all the people and the banqueters listen to a minstrel from their seats in the hall, while the tables before them are laden with bread and meat, and a steward carries round the wine he has drawn from the bowl and fills their cups. This, to my way of thinking, is perfection.

'However, your heart has prompted you to ask me about my troubles, and that intensified my grief. Well, where shall I begin, where end, my tale? For the list of woes which the gods in heaven have sent me is a long one. I shall start by giving you my name: I wish you all to know it so that in times to come, if I escape the evil day, I may always be your friend, though my home is far from here.

'I am Odysseus, Laertes' son. The whole world talks of my stratagems, and my fame has reached the heavens. My home is under the clear skies of Ithaca. Our landmark is Mount Neriton with its quivering leaves. Other islands are clustered round it, Dulichium and Same and wooded Zacynthus. But Ithaca, the farthest out to sea, lies slanting to the west, whereas the others face the dawn and rising sun. It is a rough land, but nurtures fine men. And I, for one, know of no sweeter sight for a man's eyes than his own country. The divine Calypso was certainly for keeping me in her cavern home because she yearned for me to be her husband and with the same object Circe, the Aeaean witch, detained me in her palace; but never for a moment did they win my heart. So true it is that a man's fatherland and his parents are what he holds sweetest, even though he has settled far away from his people in some rich home in foreign lands. However, let me tell you of the disastrous voyage Zeus inflicted on me when I started back from Troy.

'The same wind that wafted me from Ilium brought me to Ismarus, the city of the Cicones. I sacked this place and destroyed its menfolk. The women and the vast plunder that we took from the town we divided so that no one, as far as I could help it, should go short of his proper share. And then I said we must escape with all possible speed. But my fools of men refused. There was plenty of wine, plenty of livestock; and they kept on drinking and butchering sheep and shambling crooked-horned cattle by the shore. Meanwhile the Cicones went and raised a cry for help among other Cicones, their inland neighbours, who are both numerous and better men, trained in fighting from the chariot and on foot as well, when the occasion requires.

'At dawn they were on us, thick as the leaves and flowers in spring, and disaster, sent by Zeus to make us suffer, overtook my doomed companions and me. They fought a pitched battle by the swift ships and exchanged volleys of bronze spears.

Right through the early morning and while the blessed light of day grew stronger we held our ground and kept their greater force at bay; but when the sun began to drop, towards the time when the ploughman unyokes his ox, the Cicones gained the upper hand and broke the Achaean ranks. Six of my strong-greaved comrades from each ship were killed. The rest of us eluded our fate and got away alive.

'We sailed on from Ismarus with heavy hearts, grieving for the loss of our dear companions though rejoicing at our own escape; and I would not let the curved ships sail before each of our poor comrades who had fallen in action against the Cicones had been three times saluted with a ritual call. Zeus, who marshals the clouds, now sent my fleet a terrible gale from the north. He covered land and sea alike with a canopy of cloud; darkness swept down on us from the sky. Our ships pitched and plunged in the wind, and the force of the gusts tore their sails to shreds and tatters. With the fear of death upon us, we lowered them on to the decks, and rowed the bare ships to the land with all our might.

'We rested on land for two days and two nights on end, with exhaustion and anxiety gnawing at our hearts. But on the third morning, which bright-haired Dawn had ushered in, we stepped the masts, hauled up the white sails, and took our places in the ship. The wind and the helmsmen kept our vessels straight. In fact I should have reached my own land safe and sound, had not the swell, the current and the North Wind combined, as I was rounding Malea, to drive me off my course and send me drifting past Cythera.

'For nine days I was chased by those accursed winds across

the teeming seas. But on the tenth we reached the country of the Lotus-eaters, a race that eat the flowery lotus fruit. We disembarked to draw water, and my crews quickly had a meal by the ships. When we had eaten and drunk, I sent some of my followers inland to find out what sort of human beings might be there, detailing two men for the duty with a third as herald. Off they went, and it was not long before they came upon Lotus-eaters. Now these natives had no intention of killing my comrades; what they did was to give them some lotus to taste. Those who ate the honeyed fruit of the plant lost any wish to come back and bring us news. All they now wanted was to stay where they were with the Lotus-eaters, to browse on the lotus, and to forget all thoughts of return. I had to use force to bring them back to the hollow ships, and they wept on the way, but once on board I tied them up and dragged them under the benches. I then commanded the rest of my loyal band to embark with all speed on their fast ships, for the fear that others of them might eat the lotus and think no more of home. They came on board at once, took their places at their oars and all together struck the white surf with their blades.

'So we left that country and sailed with heavy hearts. And we came to the land of the Cyclopes, a fierce, lawless people who never lift a hand to plant or plough but just leave everything to the immortal gods. All the crops they require spring up unsown and untilled, wheat and barley and vines with generous clusters that swell with the rain from heaven to yield wine. The Cyclopes have no assemblies for the making of laws, nor any established legal codes, but live in hollow caverns in the mountain heights, where each man is lawgiver to his own children and women, and nobody has the slightest interest in what his neighbours decide.

'Not very far from the harbour of the Cyclopes' country, and not so near either, there lies a luxuriant island, covered with woods, which is the home of innumerable goats. The goats are wild, for the footsteps of man never disturb them, nor do hunters visit the island, forcing their way through forests and ranging the mountain tops. Used neither for grazing nor for ploughing, it lies for ever unsown and untilled; and this land where no man goes supports only bleating goats. The Cyclopes have nothing like our ships with their crimson prows; they have no shipwrights to build merchantmen that could give them the means of sailing across the sea to visit foreign towns and people, as other nations do. Such craftsmen would have turned the island into a fine colony for the Cyclopes.

'It is by no means a poor country, but capable of yielding any crop in due season. Along the shore of the grey sea there are lush water-meadows where the grapes would never fail; and there is land level enough for the plough, where they could count on cutting a tall-standing crop at every harvest because the subsoil is exceedingly rich. Also it has a safe harbour, in which there is no need of moorings – no need to cast anchor or make fast with hawsers: all your crew need do is beach their ship and wait till the spirit moves them and the right wind blows. Finally, at the head of the harbour there is a stream of fresh water, running out of a cave in a grove of poplar-trees.

'This is where we came to land. Some god must have guided us through the murky night, for it was impossible to see ahead. The ships were in a thick fog, and overhead not a gleam of light came through from the moon, which was obscured by clouds. Not a man among us caught sight of the island, nor did we even see the long breakers rolling up to the coast, before our good ships ran aground. It was not till they were beached that we lowered sail. We then jumped out on to the shore, fell asleep where we were and so waited for the blessed light of day.

'As soon as Dawn appeared, fresh and rosy-fingered, we were delighted with what we saw of the island, and set out to explore it. Presently the Nymphs, those children of Zeus, set the mountain goats on the move to ensure my companions a meal. Directly we saw them we fetched our curved bows and our long spears from the ships, separated into three parties, and began shooting at the goats; and in a short time the god had sent us plenty of game. When it was shared out, nine goats were allotted to each of the twelve ships under my command, but to me alone they made an allotment of ten.

'So the whole day long till the sun set we sat down to rich supplies of meat and mellow wine, since the ships had not yet run dry of our red vintage. There was still some in the holds, for when we took the sacred citadel of the Cicones, every member of the company had drawn off a generous supply in jars. There we sat, and as we looked across at the neighbouring land of the Cyclopes, we could see the smoke from their fires and hear their voices and the bleating of their sheep and goats.

The sun went down, night fell, and we lay down to sleep on the sea-shore.

'As soon as Dawn appeared, fresh and rosy-fingered, I assembled my company and spoke to them. "My good friends," I said, "for the time being stay here, while I go in my ship with my crew to find out what kind of men are over there, and whether they are aggressive savages with no sense of right or wrong or hospitable and god-fearing people."

'Then I climbed into my ship and told my men to follow me and loose the hawsers. They came on board at once, took their places at the oars and all together struck the white surf with the blades. It was no great distance to the mainland. As we approached its nearest point, we made out a cave close to the sea, with a high entrance overhung by laurels. Here large flocks of sheep and goats were penned at night, and round the mouth a yard had been built with a great wall of quarried stones and tall pines and high-branched oaks. It was the den of a giant, who pastured his flocks alone, a long way away from anyone else, and had no truck with others of his kind but lived aloof in his own lawless way. And what a formidable monster he was! He was quite unlike any man who eats bread, more like some wooded peak in the high hills, standing out alone apart from the others.

'At this point, I told the rest of my loyal companions to stay there on guard by the ship, but I myself picked out the twelve best men in the company and advanced. I took with me in a goatskin some dark and mellow wine which had been given to me by Maron, son of Euanthes, the priest of Apollo, the tutelary god of Ismarus, because we had protected him and his

7

child and wife out of respect for his office. He lived in a wooded grove sacred to Phoebus Apollo. This man had given me some fine presents: seven talents of wrought gold, with a mixing-bowl of solid silver, and he drew off for me a dozen jars of mellow unmixed wine as well. It was a wonderful drink. It had been kept a secret from all his serving-men and maids, in fact from everyone in the house but himself, his good wife and a housekeeper. To drink this red and honeyed vintage, he would pour one cupful of wine into twenty of water, and the bouquet that rose from the bowl was pure heaven – those were occasions when abstinence could have no charms.

'Well, I filled a big goatskin with this wine and also took some food in a bag with me; for I had an instant foreboding that we were going to find ourselves face to face with some barbarous being of colossal strength and ferocity, uncivilized and unprincipled. It took us very little time to reach the cave, but we did not find its owner at home: he was tending his fat sheep in the pastures. So we went inside and looked in amazement at everything. There were baskets laden with cheeses, and the folds were thronged with lambs and kids, each group – the spring ones, the summer ones, and new-born ones – being separately penned. All his well-made vessels, the pails and bowls for he used for milking, were swimming with whey.

'To start with my men begged me to let them take away some of the cheeses, then come back, drive the kids and lambs quickly out of the pens down to the good ship, and so set sail across the salt water. But though it would have been far better so I was not to be persuaded. I wished to see the owner of the cave and had hopes of some friendly gifts from my host. But when he did appear, my men were not going to find him a very likeable character.

'We lit a fire, made an offering to the gods, helped ourselves to some of the cheeses, and when we had eaten, sat down in the cave to await his arrival. At last he came up, shepherding his flocks and carrying a huge bundle of dry wood to burn at supper-time. With a great crash he threw this down inside the cavern, giving us such a fright that we hastily retreated to an inner recess. Meanwhile he drove some of his fat flock into the wider part of the cave – all the ones he was milking – the rams and he-goats he left out of doors in the walled yard. He then picked up a huge stone, with which he closed the entrance. It was a mighty slab; twenty-two four-wheeled waggons could not shift such a massive stone from the entrance, such was the monstrous size of the rock with which he closed the cave. Next he sat down to milk his ewes and his bleating goats, which he did methodically, putting her young to each mother as he finished. He then curdled half the white milk, collected the whey, and stored it in wicker cheese-baskets; the remainder he left standing in pails, so that it would be handy at supper-time when he wanted a drink. When he had efficiently finished his tasks, he re-lit the fire and spied us.

'"Strangers!" he cried. "And who are you? Where do you come from over the watery ways? Is yours a trading venture; or are you cruising the main on chance, like roving pirates, who risk their lives to ruin other people?"

'Our hearts sank. The booming voice and the very sight of

the monster filled us with panic. Still, I managed to find words to answer him. "We are Achaeans," I said, "on our way back from Troy – driven astray by contrary winds across a vast expanse of sea – we're making our way home but took the wrong way – the wrong route – as Zeus, I suppose, intended that we should. We are proud to say that we belong to the forces of Agamemnon, Atreus' son, who by sacking the great city of Ilium and destroying all its armies has made himself the most famous man in the world today. We find ourselves here as suppliants at your knees, in the hope that you may give us hospitality, or even give us the kind of gifts that hosts customarily give their guests. Good sir, remember your duty to the gods; we are your suppliants, and Zeus is the champion of suppliants and guests. He is the god of guests: guests are sacred to him, and he goes alongside them."

'That is what I said, and he answered me promptly out of his pitiless heart: "Stranger, you must be a fool, or must have come from very far afield, to order me to fear or reverence the gods. We Cyclopes care nothing for Zeus with his aegis, nor for the rest of the blessed gods, since we are much stronger than they are. I would never spare you or your men for fear of incurring Zeus' enmity, unless I felt like it. But tell me where you moored your good ship when you came. Was it somewhere along the coast, or nearby? I'd like to know."

'His words were designed to get the better of me, but he could not outwit someone with my knowledge of the world. I answered with plausible words: "As for my ship, it was wrecked by the Earthshaker Poseidon on the borders of your land. The wind had carried us on to a lee shore. He drove the ship up to a headland and hurled it on the rocks. But I and my friends here managed to escape with our lives."

'To this the cruel brute made no reply. Instead, he jumped up, and reaching out towards my men, seized a couple and dashed their heads against the floor as though they had been puppies. Their brains ran out on the ground and soaked the earth. Limb by limb he tore them to pieces to make his meal, which he devoured like a mountain lion, leaving nothing, neither entrails nor flesh, marrow nor bones, while we, weeping, lifted up our hands to Zeus in horror at the ghastly sight. We felt completely helpless. When the Cyclops had filled his great belly with this meal of human flesh, which he washed down with unwatered milk, he stretched himself out for sleep among his flocks inside the cave.

'On first thoughts I planned to summon my courage, draw my sharp sword from the scabbard at my side, creep up to him, feel for the right place with my hand and stab him in the breast where the liver is supported by the midriff. But on second thoughts I refrained, realizing that we would seal our own fate as well as his, because we would have found it impossible with our unaided hands to push aside the huge rock with which he had closed the great mouth of the cave. So with sighs and groans we waited for the blessed light of day.

'As soon as Dawn appeared, fresh and rosy-fingered, the Cyclops re-lit the fire and milked his splendid ewes and goats, all in their proper order, putting her young to each. Having efficiently completed all these tasks, he once more snatched up a couple of my men and prepared his meal. When he had eaten, he turned his plump flocks out of the cave, removing the great doorstone without effort. But he replaced it once more, as though he were putting the lid on a quiver. Then, with frequent whistles, he drove his plump flocks off towards the mountain, and I was left, with murder in my heart, scheming how to pay him out if only Athene would grant me my prayer. The best plan I could think of was this.

'Lying by the pen the Cyclops had a huge staff of green olive-wood, which he had cut to carry in his hand when it was seasoned. To us it looked more like the mast of some black ship of twenty oars, a broad-bottomed merchantman such as makes long sea-voyages. That was the impression which its length and thickness made on us. Standing beside this piece of timber I cut off a fathom's length, which I handed over to my men and told them to smooth it down. When they had done this I stood and sharpened it to a point. Then I hardened it in the fire, and finally I carefully hid it under the dung, of which there were great heaps scattered throughout the cave. I then told my company to cast lots for the dangerous task of helping me to lift the pole and twist it in the Cyclops' eye when he was sound asleep. The lot fell on the very men that I myself would have chosen, four of them, so that counting myself we made a party of five.

'Evening came, and with it the Cyclops, shepherding his plump flocks, every one of which he herded into the broad cave, leaving none out in the walled yard, either because he suspected something or because a god had ordered him to. He lifted the great doorstone, set it in its place, and then sat down to milk his ewes and bleating goats, which he did methodically, giving each mother its young one in due course. When he had efficiently completed all these tasks, he once more snatched two of us and prepared his supper. Then with an ivy-wood bowl of my dark wine in my hands, I went up to him and said: "Here, Cyclops, have some wine to wash down that meal of human flesh, and find out for yourself what kind of vintage was stored away in our ship's hold. I brought it for you as an offering in the hope that you would take pity on me and help me on my homeward way. But your savagery is more than we can bear. Hard-hearted man, how can you expect ever to have a visitor again from the world of men? You have not behaved rightly."

'The Cyclops took the wine and drank it up. And the delicious drink gave him such exquisite pleasure that he asked me for another bowlful. "Give me more, please, and tell me your name, here and now – I would like to make you a gift that will please you. We Cyclopes have wine of our own made from the grapes that our rich soil and rains from Zeus produce. But this vintage of yours is a drop of the real nectar and ambrosia."

'So said the Cyclops, and I handed him another bowlful of the sparkling wine. Three times I filled it for him; and three times the fool drained the bowl to the dregs. At last, when the wine had fuddled his wits, I addressed him with soothing words.

'"Cyclops," I said, "you ask me my name. I'll tell it to you; and in return give me the gift you promised me. My name is Nobody. That is what I am called by my mother and father and by all my friends."

'The Cyclops answered me from his cruel heart. "Of all his

company I will eat Nobody last, and the rest before him. That shall be your gift."

'He had hardly spoken before he toppled over and fell face upwards on the floor, where he lay with his great neck twisted to one side, and all-compelling sleep overpowered him. In his drunken stupor he vomited, and a stream of wine mixed with morsels of men's flesh poured from his throat. I went at once and thrust our pole deep under the ashes of the fire to make it hot, and meanwhile gave a word of encouragement to all my men, to make sure that no one would hang back through fear. When the fierce glow from the olive stake warned me that it was about to catch alight in the flames, green as it was, I withdrew it from the fire and my men gathered round. A god now inspired them with tremendous courage. Seizing the olive pole, they drove its sharpened end into the Cyclops' eye, while I used my weight from above to twist it home, like a man boring a ship's timber with a drill which his mates below him twirl with a strap they hold at either end, so that it spins continuously. In much the same way we handled our pole with its red-hot point and twisted it in his eye till the blood boiled up round the burning wood. The scorching heat singed his lids and brow all round, while his eyeball blazed and the very roots crackled in the flame. The Cyclops' eye hissed round the olive stake in the same way that an axe or adze hisses when a smith plunges it into cold water to quench and strengthen the iron. He gave a dreadful shriek, which echoed round the rocky walls, and we backed away from him in terror, while he pulled the stake from his eye, streaming with blood. Then he hurled it away from him with frenzied hands and raised a great shout to the other Cyclopes who lived in neighbouring caves along the windy heights. Hearing his screams they came up from every quarter, and gathering outside the cave asked him what the matter was.

'"What on earth is wrong with you, Polyphemus? Why must you disturb the peaceful night and spoil our sleep with all this shouting? Is a robber driving off your sheep, or is somebody trying by treachery or violence to kill you?"

'Out of the cave came mighty Polyphemus' voice in reply: "O my friends, it's Nobody's treachery, not violence, that is doing me to death."

'"Well then," came the immediate reply, "if you are alone and nobody is assaulting you, you must be sick and sickness comes from almighty Zeus and cannot be helped. All you can do is to pray to your father, the Lord Poseidon."

'And off they went, while I laughed to myself at the way in which my cunning *notion** of a false name had taken them in. The Cyclops, still moaning in agonies of pain, groped about with his hands and pushed the rock away from the mouth of the cave. Then he sat himself down in the doorway and stretched out both arms in the hope of catching us in the act of slipping out among the sheep. What a fool he must have thought me! Meanwhile I was cudgelling my brains for the best possible course, trying to hit on some way of saving my friends as well as myself. I thought up plan after plan, scheme

* The Greek for 'no one' is *me tis*, but run together as *metis* it means 'wily scheme, resourcefulness'. Odysseus laughs to himself because *metis* (no one/resourcefulness) has foiled the Cyclops. 'Notion' is an attempt to get the pun.

after scheme. It was a matter of life or death: we were in mortal peril.

'This was the scheme that eventually seemed best. The rams of the flock were of good stock, thick-fleeced, fine, big animals in their coats of black wool. These I quietly lashed together with the plaited willow twigs which the inhuman monster used for his bed. I took them in threes. The middle one was to carry one of my followers, with its fellows on either side to protect him. Each of my men thus had three rams to bear him. But for myself I chose a full-grown ram who was the pick of the whole flock. Seizing him by the back, I curled myself up under his shaggy belly and lay there upside down, with a firm grip on his wonderful fleece and with patience in my heart. In this way, with sighs and groans, we waited for the blessed Dawn.

'As soon as she arrived, fresh and rosy-fingered, the he-goats and the rams began to scramble out and make for the pastures, but the females, unmilked as they were and with udders full to bursting, stood bleating by the pens. Their master, though tortured and in terrible agony, passed his hands along the backs of all the animals as they stopped in front of him; but the idiot never noticed that my men were tied under the chests of his own woolly rams. The last of the flock to come up to the doorway was the big ram, burdened by his own fleece and by me with my thoughts racing. As he felt him with his hands the great Polyphemus broke into speech:

'"Sweet ram," he said, "why are you the last of the flock to pass out of the cave like this? You have never before lagged behind the others, but always step so proudly out and are the first of them to crop the lush shoots of the grass, first to make your way to the flowing stream, and first to want to return to the fold when evening falls. Yet today you are the last of all. You must be grieved for your master's eye, blinded by a wicked man and his accursed friends, when he had robbed me of my wits with wine. Nobody was his name; and I swear that he has not yet saved his skin! Ah, if only you could feel as I do and find a voice to tell me where he's hiding from my fury! I'd hammer him and splash his brains all over the floor of the cave, and my heart would find some relief from the suffering which that nothing, that Nobody, has caused me!"

'So he let the ram pass through the entrance and when we had put a little distance between ourselves and the courtyard of the cave, I first let go my ram and then untied my men. Then, quickly, though with many a backward look, we drove our long-striding sheep and goats – a rich, fat flock – right down to the ship. My dear companions were overjoyed when they caught sight of us survivors, but broke into loud lamentations for the others. With nods and frowns I indicated silently that they should stop their weeping and hurry to bundle the fleecy sheep and goats on board and put to sea. So they went on board at once, took their places at the oars, and all together struck the white water with the blades.

'But before we were out of earshot, I shouted out derisive words at Polyphemus. "Cyclops! So he was not such a weakling after all, the man whose friends you meant to overpower and eat in your hollow cave! And your crimes were bound to catch up with you, you brute, who did not shrink from

17

devouring your guests. Now Zeus and all the other gods have paid you out."

'My words so enraged the Cyclops that he tore the top off a great pinnacle of rock and hurled it at us. The rock fell just ahead of our blue-painted bows. As it plunged in, the water surged up and the backwash, like a swell from the open sea, swept us landward and nearly drove us on to the beach. Seizing a long pole, I pushed the ship off, at the same time commanding my crew with urgent nods to bend to their oars and save us from disaster. They leant forward and rowed with a will; but when they had taken us across the water to twice our previous distance I was about to shout something else to the Cyclops, but from all parts of the ship my men called out, trying to restrain and pacify me.

'"Why do you want to provoke the savage in this obstinate way? The rock he threw into the sea just now drove the ship back to the land, and we thought it was all up with us. Had he heard a cry, or so much as a word, from a single man, he'd have smashed in our heads and the ship's timbers with another jagged boulder from his hand. We're within easy range for him!"

'But my temper was up; their words did not dissuade me, and in my rage I shouted back at him once more: "Cyclops, if anyone ever asks you how you came by your blindness, tell him your eye was put out by Odysseus, sacker of cities, the son of Laertes, who lives in Ithaca."

'The Cyclops gave a groan. "Alas!" he cried. "Those ancient prophecies have come back to me now! We had a prophet living with us once, a great and mighty man, Eurymus' son

Telemus, the best of soothsayers, who grew old as a seer among us Cyclopes. All that has now happened he foretold, when he warned me that a man called Odysseus would rob me of my sight. But I always expected some big handsome man of tremendous strength to come along. And now, a puny, feeble good-for-nothing fuddles me with wine and then puts out my eye! But come here, Odysseus, so that I can give you some friendly gifts and prevail on the great Earthshaker, Poseidon, to see you safely home. For I am his son, and he is proud to call himself my father. He is the one who will heal me if he's willing – a thing no other blessed god nor any man on earth could do."

'To which I shouted in reply: "I only wish I could make as sure of robbing you of life and breath and sending you to Hell, as I am certain that not even the Earthshaker will ever heal your eye."

'At this the Cyclops lifted up his hands to the starry heavens and prayed to the Lord Poseidon: "Hear me, Poseidon, Sustainer of the Earth, god of the sable locks. If I am yours indeed and you claim me as your son, grant that Odysseus, sacker of cities and son of Laertes, may never reach his home in Ithaca. But if he is destined to see his friends again, to come once more to his own house and reach his native land, let him come late, in wretched plight, having lost all his comrades, in a foreign ship, and let him find trouble in his home."

'So Polyphemus prayed; and the god of the sable locks heard his prayer. Once again the Cyclops picked up a boulder – bigger, by far, this time – and hurled it with a swing, putting such tremendous force into his throw that the rock fell only just astern of our blue-painted ship, narrowly missing the tip of the rudder. The water heaved up as it plunged into the sea; but the wave that it raised carried us on toward the further shore.

'And so we reached our island, where the rest of our good ships were all waiting for us, their crews sitting round disconsolate and keeping a constant watch for our return. Once there, we beached our ship, jumped out on the shore, and unloaded the Cyclops' flocks from the hold. We then divided our spoil so that no one, as far as I could help it, should go short of his proper share. But my comrades-in-arms did me the special honour, when the sheep and goats were distributed, of presenting me with the big ram in addition. Him I sacrificed on the beach, burning slices from his thighs as an offering to Zeus of the Black Clouds, the Son of Cronos, who is lord of us all. But Zeus took no notice of my sacrifice; his mind must already have been full of plans for the destruction of all my fine ships and of my loyal band.

'So the whole day long till sundown we sat and feasted on our rich supply of meat and mellow wine. When the sun set and darkness fell, we lay down to sleep on the sea-shore. As soon as Dawn appeared, fresh and rosy-fingered, I roused my men and ordered them to go on board and cast off. They climbed on board at once, took their places at the oars and all together struck the white surf with the blades. Thus we left the island and sailed on with heavy hearts, grieving for the dear friends we had lost but glad at our own escape from death.'

Circe

'We next came to the floating island of Aeolia, the home of Aeolus son of Hippotas, who is a favourite of the immortal gods. All round this isle there runs an unbroken wall of bronze, and below it the cliffs rise sheer from the sea. Aeolus shares his house with his family of twelve, six daughters and six grown-up sons; and he has given his daughters to his sons in marriage. With their father and their estimable mother they are always feasting. Countless delicacies are laid out before them, and all day long the house is filled with the savoury smell of roasting meat, and the courtyard echoes to the sounds of banqueting within. At night they sleep, each with his loving wife, on ornate beds, with plenty of rugs.

'To this domain of theirs and this magnificent palace we now came. For a whole month Aeolus entertained me and questioned me on everything – Troy, the Achaean navy and our return – and I told him everything, exactly as it was. When it came to my turn and I asked him whether I might now continue my journey and count on his help, he gave it willingly. He made arrangements for my journey and presented me with a leather bag, made from the flayed skin of a full-grown ox, in which he had imprisoned the boisterous energies of all the winds. Zeus had put him in charge of the winds, with power to lay or rouse them each at will. This bag he stowed in the hold of my ship, securing it tightly with a burnished silver wire to prevent the slightest leakage. Then he called up a breeze from the west to blow my ships and their crews across the sea. But his measures were doomed to failure, for we came to grief, through our own senseless stupidity.

'For nine days and nights we sailed on; and on the tenth we were already in sight of our homeland, and had even come near enough to see people tending their fires, when I fell fast asleep. I was utterly exhausted, for in my anxiety to speed our journey home I handled the sheet of my ship myself without a break, giving it to no one else.

'The crew began to discuss matters among themselves, and word went round that I was bringing home a fortune in gold and silver which the great-hearted Aeolus son of Hippotas had given me. And this is what they said as they exchanged glances: "It's not fair! What a captain we have, valued wherever he goes and welcomed in every port! Back he comes from Troy with a splendid haul of plunder, though we who have gone every bit as far come home with empty hands – and now Aeolus has given him all this into the bargain, as a favour for friendship's sake! Come on; let's find out and see how much gold and silver is hidden in that bag."

'After talk like this evil counsels prevailed. They undid the bag, the winds all rushed out, and in an instant the tempest was upon them, carrying them headlong out to sea, in tears, away from their native land. When I awoke my spirit failed me. I debated within myself whether to jump overboard and drown or stay among the living and quietly endure. I stayed and endured. Covering my head with my cloak, I lay where I

22

was in the ship. So all my ships, with their distraught crews, were driven back to the island of Aeolus.

'We disembarked and collected water, and the men straightaway had a quick meal by the ships. But as soon as we had had something to eat and drink I took a messenger and one of my comrades to accompany me and set out for the palace of Aeolus, whom we found at dinner with his wife and family. We went in and sat down on the threshold by the door-posts.

'They were astounded at the sight of us. "Odysseus?" they exclaimed. "How do *you* come to be here? What evil power has dealt this blow? We did our best to help you on your way home to Ithaca or any port you might choose."

'I replied sorrowfully, "An untrustworthy crew and a fatal sleep were my downfall. Put things right for me, my friends. You easily could." It was with these placatory words that I appealed to them.

'They remained silent. Then the father answered. "Get off this island instantly! The world holds no one more damnable than you, and it is not right for me to entertain and equip a man detested by the blessed gods. Your returning like this *shows* they detest you. Get out!"

'Thus he dismissed me from his palace, causing me deep distress. We left the island and resumed our journey in a state of gloom; and the heart was taken out of my men by the wearisome rowing. But it was our own stupidity that had deprived us of the wind.

'For six days and six nights we sailed on, and on the seventh we came to Telepylus, Lamus' stronghold in the Laestrygonian land, where herdsmen bringing in their flocks at night exchange greetings with other herdsmen driving out at dawn. For in this land nightfall and morning tread so closely on each other's heels that a man who could do without sleep might earn two wages, one for herding cattle and the other for shepherding flocks of white sheep. Here we found an excellent harbour, closed in on all sides by an unbroken ring of precipitous cliffs, with two jutting headlands facing each other at the mouth so as to leave only a narrow channel in between.

'The captains of my squadron all steered their curved craft straight into the harbour and tied up in the sheltered waters within. They remained close together, for it was obvious that there was never any swell there, slight or strong, but always a flat calm. But I did not follow them. Instead I brought my black ship to rest outside the harbour and made her fast with a cable to a rock at the end of the point. I then climbed the headland to get a view from the top. But no cultivated fields or herds of cattle were visible; all we saw was a wisp of smoke rising up from the countryside. So I sent a party inland to find out what sort of people the inhabitants were, two of my men, together with a messenger.

'When they had left the ships they found a well-worn track used by waggons bringing timber down from the high mountains to the town. Presently they came across a strong girl drawing water outside the town, the daughter of Antiphates, the Laestrygonian chief. She had come down to a bubbling spring called Artacie, from which the townspeople drew their water. When they went up and asked her who the ruler of the country was and what his people were called, she pointed at once to the high roof of her father's dwelling. When they entered his palace they were confronted by Antiphates' wife, a woman of mountainous proportions; the sight of her appalled them. She called her husband, the famous Antiphates, from the assembly-place, who promptly made his murderous intentions clear, pouncing on one of my men to eat him for supper. The other two sprang back and fled, and managed to make their way back to the ships.

'Meanwhile Antiphates raised a hue and cry through the town, which brought countless numbers of powerful Laestrygonians running up from every side, more like Giants than men. Standing at the top of the cliffs they began pelting my flotilla with lumps of rock such as an ordinary man could barely lift; and the din that now rose from the ships, where the groans of dying men could be heard above the splintering of timbers, was appalling. They carried them off like fishes on a spear to make their loathsome meal. But while this massacre was still going on in the deep harbour, I drew my sword from my hip, slashed through the hawser of my blue-prowed vessel, and shouted to the crew to bend to their oars if they wished to save their lives. With the fear of death upon them they struck the water like one man, and to our relief and joy we shot out to sea and left those frowning cliffs behind. My ship was safe. But that was the end of all the rest.

'We travelled on with heavy hearts, grieving for the loss of our dear friends though rejoicing at our own escape. In due course we came to the island of Aeaea, the home of the beautiful Circe, a formidable goddess, with a mortal woman's voice. She is the sister of the baleful Aeetes, both being children of the Sun who lights the world, by the same mother, Perse the Daughter of Ocean. We brought our ship into the shelter of the harbour without a sound. Some god guided us in. And when we disembarked, we lay on the beach for two days and nights, utterly exhausted and eating our hearts out with grief.

'When Dawn with her beautiful tresses ushered in the third day, I took my spear and sword, left the ship, and struck inland, making for a vantage-point from which I might see signs of cultivation or hear men's voices. I climbed to a rocky height, and on reaching the top I was able to see the smoke rising from the distant place where Circe's house lay in a clearing among the dense oak-scrub and forest trees. That glimpse I had of reddish smoke left me in two minds whether or not to press forward and reconnoitre. After some thought I decided the better course would be to return to my ship on the beach, give my men a meal, and send out an exploring party.

'And then some god was moved to pity by my forlorn condition. For when I had almost reached the ship, he sent a great antlered stag right across my path. The fierce heat of the sun had driven him down from the forest pastures to drink at a stream, and as he came up from the water I struck him on the spine half-way down his back. My bronze spear went right through him, and with a bellow he fell in the dust and was dead. With one foot on his carcass I dragged the bronze spear out of the wound, laid it on the ground, and left it there while I broke off creepers and shoots from undergrowth and willows, which I twisted into a fathom's length of rope carefully plaited from end to end. With this I tied the monster's feet together, and slinging him around my neck, I made for the ship, using my spear as a staff. I could not possibly have balanced him on one shoulder with my free hand – he was a massive brute. When I reached the ship, I threw the stag down in front of it, and going up to each man in turn heartened them with a cheerful word.

'"My friends," I said "we may be miserable, but we are not going down to the house of Hades yet, not till our time has come. Get up, and while there's food and drink on board, let us have something to eat instead of dying here of starvation."

'This was advice they took readily enough. They at once flung off their rugs, and there on the desolate sea-shore they gazed open-mouthed at the stag; he really was a monster. When they had feasted their eyes on the sight they washed their hands and prepared a glorious meal. So the whole day long till sundown we sat down to a feast of unlimited meat and mellow wine. When the sun set and darkness fell, we lay down to sleep on the sea-shore. As soon as Dawn appeared, fresh and rosy-fingered, I gathered my men round me and addressed them.

'"Comrades in suffering, friends, listen to me. We are utterly lost. We do not know where east or west is; where the light-giving Sun rises or where he sets. So the sooner we decide on a sensible plan the better – if one can still be found, which I doubt. For when I climbed the crag I found that this is an island, and low-lying; all round it in a ring the sea stretches away to the horizon. But what I did see, right in the middle, through dense oak-scrub and forest, was a wisp of smoke."

'When they heard my report they broke down completely. They could not help remembering what Antiphates the Laestrygonian had done, and the unbridled savagery of the maneating Cyclops. They burst into loud sobs and the tears streamed down their cheeks. But they might have spared themselves their lamentations for all the good they did.

'In the end I divided my well-armed crew into two parties with a leader for each. Of one party I myself took charge; the other I gave to the noble Eurylochus. Then we shook lots in a bronze helmet and out jumped the lot of the great-hearted Eurylochus, so he went off with his twenty-two men, a tearful company, leaving us, who stayed behind, weeping too. In a clearing, in a glade they came upon Circe's house, built of polished stone. Prowling about the place were mountain wolves and lions that Circe had bewitched with her magic drugs. They did not attack my men, but rose on their hind legs to fawn on them, with much wagging of their long tails, like dogs fawning on their master as he comes from table for the tasty bits he always brings. In the same way these wolves and lions with great claws fawned round my men. Terrified at the sight of the formidable beasts, they stood in the palace porch of the goddess with the lovely tresses. They could hear Circe within, singing in her beautiful voice as she went to and fro at her great and everlasting loom, on which she was weaving one of those delicate, graceful and dazzling fabrics that goddesses make.

'Polites, an authoritative man and the one in my party whom I liked and trusted most, now took the lead. "Friends," he said, "there is someone in the castle working at a loom.

The whole place echoes to that lovely voice. It's either a goddess or a woman. Let us call to her immediately."

'So they called and Circe came out at once, opened the polished doors, and invited them to enter. In their innocence, the whole party followed her in. But Eurylochus suspected a trap and stayed outside. Circe ushered the rest into her hall, gave them seats and chairs to sit on, and then prepared them a mixture of cheese, barley-meal, and yellow honey flavoured with Pramnian wine. But into this dish she introduced a noxious drug, to make them lose all memory of their native land. And when they had emptied the bowls which she had handed them, she drove them with blows of a stick into the pigsties. Now they had pigs' heads and bristles, and they grunted like pigs; but their minds were as human as they had been before. So, weeping, they were penned in their sties. Then Circe flung them some forest nuts, acorns and cornel-berries – the usual food of pigs that wallow in the mud.

'Meanwhile Eurylochus came back to the swift black ship to report the catastrophe his party had met with. He was in such anguish that he could not utter a single word; his eyes were filled with tears, and he felt on the verge of breaking down. Exasperated, we all bombarded him with questions, till at length he came out with the story of his comrades' fate.

'"We went – as you ordered – through the woods – noble Odysseus. In a clearing, in a glade, we came to a well-built house of polished stone. Someone inside was singing in a clear voice as she went to and fro at her great web – either a goddess or a woman. My men called and she came out, immediately opened the polished doors, and invited us to enter. In their innocence, the whole party followed her in. But I suspected a trap and stayed outside. And now the whole party has been wiped out. Not a single man reappeared, though I sat there a long time, watching."

'When I heard this story I slung my big bronze silver-studded sword in its silver scabbard over my shoulder, then my bow, and I told Eurylochus to take me back with him by the way he had come. But he threw his arms round my knees in supplication and broke into a pitiful appeal.

'"Favourite of Zeus," he said, "leave me behind; don't force me to go with you there. You will never come back yourself and you won't rescue a single man of your crew. I am certain of it. Let us get away quickly with those that are left here. We might still escape the evil day."

'"Very well, Eurylochus," I replied; "stay were you are, and eat and drink by the black ship's hull. But I shall go. I have absolutely no choice."

'With this, I turned my back on the ship and the sea, and struck inland. But, threading my way through the enchanted glades, I was nearing the sorceress's palace when I met Hermes, god of the golden wand, looking like a young man at that most charming age when the beard first starts to grow. He took my hand in his and greeted me amiably.

'"Where are you off to now, my poor fellow," he said, "wandering alone through the wilds in unknown country, with your friends in Circe's house penned like pigs in their crowded sties? Have you come here to free them? I think you are more likely to stay with them yourself and never see your home. However, I will save you and deliver you from your trouble. Look: here is a drug of real virtue that you must take with you into Circe's palace; it will make you immune from evil. I will tell you how she works her black magic. She will begin by preparing you a mixture, into which she will put her drug. But even with its help she will be unable to enchant you, for this antidote that I am going to give you will rob it of its power. I will tell you exactly what to do. When Circe strikes you with her long stick, you must draw your sword from your side and rush at her as though you mean to kill her. She will shrink from you in terror and invite you to her bed. You must not refuse the goddess's favours, if you want her to free your men and look after you. But make her swear a solemn oath by the blessed gods not to try any more of her tricks on you, or when she has you stripped naked she may rob you of your courage and your manhood."

'Then the Giant-killer handed me a herb he had plucked from the ground, and showed me what it was like. It had a black root and a milk-white flower. The gods call it moly, and it is a dangerous plant for mortal men to dig up. But the gods, after all, can do anything.

'Hermes went off through the island forest, making for high Olympus, while I with a heart oppressed by many dark forebodings pursued my way to Circe's home. I stood at the doors of the lovely goddess's palace and called out. Circe heard me, came out immediately, and, opening the polished doors, invited me in. Filled with misgivings, I followed her indoors and she offered me a beautiful silver-studded chair with a stool for my feet. She prepared a brew in a golden bowl for me to drink and with evil in her heart dropped in the drug.

She gave me the bowl and I drained it, but without suffering any magic effects. She struck me with her stick and shouted, "Off to the pigsty, and lie down with your friends." Whereupon I snatched my keen sword from my hip and rushed at Circe as though I meant to kill her. But with a shriek she slipped below my blade, clasped my knees and burst into tears.

'"Who are you and where do you come from?" she asked, and her words had wings. "Where is your native town? Who are your parents? I am amazed to see you take my drug and suffer no magic change. For never before have I known a man who could resist that drug once he had taken it and swallowed it down. You must have a heart in your breast that is proof against all enchantment. I am sure you are Odysseus, that resourceful man; the man whom the Giant-killer with the golden wand always told me to expect here on his way back from Troy in his swift black ship. But now put up your sword and come with me to my bed, so that in making love we may learn to trust one another."

'"Circe," I answered her, "how can you order me to be gentle with you, you who have turned my friends into pigs here in your house, and now that you have me too in your clutches are inveigling me to your bedroom and inviting me into your bed, to strip me naked and rob me of my courage and manhood? Nothing, goddess, would induce me to come into your bed unless you can bring yourself to swear a solemn oath that you have no other mischief in store for me."

'Circe at once swore as I ordered her. So when she had duly sworn the oath, I went with the goddess to her beautiful bed.

'Meanwhile the four maids who do the housework for Circe were busying themselves in the palace. They are the daughters of Springs and Groves and sacred Rivers that flow out into the sea. One of them threw linen covers over the chairs and spread fine purple rugs on top. Another drew silver tables up to the chairs and placed golden dishes upon them; the third mixed the sweet and mellow wine in a silver bowl and set out the golden cups; and the fourth fetched water and lit a fire under the big cauldron, and the water grew warm.

'When the shining bronze vessel was boiling, she sat me in a bath and washed me with water from the great cauldron mixed with cold to a comfortable heat, sluicing my head and shoulders till all the painful weariness was gone from my limbs. My bath done, she rubbed me with olive-oil, clothed me in a tunic and a splendid cloak, and seated me on a beautiful silver-studded chair with a foot-stool beneath. Next came another maid with water in a splendid golden ewer. She poured it out over a silver basin so that I could rinse my hands, and then drew up a polished table to my side. A trusty housekeeper brought some bread, which she put by me with a variety of delicacies; and after helping me liberally to all she could offer she invited me to eat. But I had no heart for eating. As I sat there my thoughts were elsewhere and my mind was full of forebodings.

'When Circe saw me sitting so quiet and not helping myself to the food, she knew that I was in deep anguish. So she came and stood by me and said with words that flew:

'"Odysseus, why are you sitting like this as though you

were dumb, and feeding on your own thoughts instead of helping yourself to meat and wine? Do you suspect another trap? You need have no fears: I have given you a solemn oath to do you no harm."

'"Circe," I answered her, "could any honourable man bear to taste food and drink before he had freed his men and seen them face to face? If you are sincere in asking me to eat and drink, give them their liberty and let me set eyes on my loyal followers."

'Stick in hand, Circe went straight out of the hall, threw open the pigsty gate, and drove them out, looking exactly like full-grown swine. When they were all in front of her she went in among them and smeared them each in turn with some new ointment. Then the bristles which her first deadly potion had caused to sprout dropped off their limbs, and they became men again and looked younger and much more handsome and taller than before. They recognized me now, and one after the other seized my hand. We were so moved that we all wept tears of happiness, till the walls echoed with the mournful sound. Even the goddess felt pity, and came to me and said: "Favourite of Zeus, son of Laertes, Odysseus of the many devices, go down now to your ship by the sea-shore, drag her straightaway on to dry land, stow your possessions and all the ship's tackle in a cave, and then come back yourself with the rest of your loyal company."

'At this my proud heart was convinced. I went to the ship and the sea-shore. I found my good companions by the ship, lamenting pitifully, with the tears streaming down their cheeks. But as soon as they caught sight of me they were all round me in a weeping throng. It was like the scene at a farm when cows in a drove come home full-fed from the pastures to the yard and are welcomed by all their frisking calves, who burst out from the pens to gambol round their mothers, lowing excitedly. My men were as deeply moved as if they had reached their homeland and were standing in their own town in rugged Ithaca, where they were born and bred.

'"Favourite of Zeus," they said between their sobs, "we are as happy to see you back as we would be to set foot on our own island of Ithaca. But tell us how our comrades met their end."

'I gave them a soothing reply. "Our first business," I said, "is to drag up the ship on to dry land and stow our possessions and the tackle in a cave. Then you must get ready and all come with me and see your friends eating and drinking in Circe's enchanted palace, where they have enough to last them for ever."

'They were quick to be convinced by my suggestion. Only Eurylochus was against me and did his best to keep the whole company back. "Where are we poor wretches off to now?" he cried with winged words. "Why are you looking for trouble – going to Circe's palace, where she will turn you all into pigs or wolves or lions, and force you to keep watch over that great house of hers? We have had all this before, with the Cyclops, when our friends found their way into his fold with this foolhardy Odysseus. It was this man's reckless folly that cost *them* their lives."

'Now when Eurylochus said that, I considered drawing the long sword from my sturdy side and lopping his head off to roll in the dust, even though he was a close kinsman of mine. But my men held me back and calmed me down.

'"Favourite of Zeus," they said, "let's leave this man here to guard the ship, if that is your order. But you lead us to Circe's enchanted castle."

'So they left the ship and the sea and struck inland. Eurylochus came with us after all. He was not going to be left by the ship; he was afraid of the stinging rebuke I might give him.

'Circe meanwhile had graciously bathed the members of my party in her palace and rubbed them with olive-oil. She gave them all tunics and warm cloaks to wear, so that on our arrival we found them having dinner together in the hall. When the two companies came face to face and they all recognized each other, they burst into tears and the whole house echoed to their sobs. But then the goddess approached me.

'"Heaven-born son of Laertes," she said, "resourceful Odysseus, check this immoderate grief. I know as well as you all you have gone through on the teeming seas and suffered at the hands of savages on land. But now eat your food and drink your wine, till you are once more the men you were when first you sailed from your homes in rugged Ithaca. You are worn out and dispirited, always brooding on the hardships of your travels. Your sufferings have been so continuous that you have lost all pleasure in living."

'My gallant company were not difficult to persuade. We stayed on day after day for a whole year, feasting on lavish quantities of meat and mellow wine. But as the months went by and the seasons passed and the long days returned, my loyal companions called me aside one day and said: "What possesses you to stay on here? It's time you thought of Ithaca, if the gods mean you to escape and get back to your ancestral home in your own country." This was enough: my proud heart was convinced.

'For the rest of that day till sunset we sat and feasted on lavish quantities of meat and mellow wine. When the sun sank and night fell, my men settled down for sleep in the darkened hall. But I went to Circe's beautiful bed and there clasped the goddess's knees in supplication, and she listened to my winged words:

'"Circe," I said, "keep that promise which you once made me, to send me home. I am eager now to be gone, and so are all my men. Whenever you are not present they stand around and exhaust me with their complaints."

'"Heaven-born son of Laertes, resourceful Odysseus," the goddess answered me, "do not stay on unwillingly. But first you have to make another journey and find your way to the Halls of Hades and dread Persephóne, to consult the soul of Teiresias, the blind Theban prophet. His faculties are unimpaired, for dead though he is, Persephone has granted him, and him alone, continuing wisdom. The others there are mere shadows flitting to and fro."

'This news broke my heart. Sitting there on the bed I wept. I had no further use for life, no wish to see the sunshine any more. But when at last I had satisfied my need for tears and for tossing and turning on the bed, I began to question her: "Circe, who is to guide me on the way? No one has ever sailed a black ship into Hell."

'"Heaven-born son of Laertes, resourceful Odysseus," the goddess answered me, "do not think of lingering on shore for lack of a pilot. Set up your mast, spread the white sail and sit down in the ship. The North Wind will blow her on her way; and when she has brought you across the River of Ocean, you will come to a wild coast and Persephone's Grove, where the tall poplars grow, and the willows that so quickly shed their seeds. Beach your boat there by Ocean's swirling stream and go on into Hade's Kingdom of Decay. There, at a rocky pinnacle, the River of Flaming Fire and the River of Lamentation, which is a branch of the Waters of Styx, meet and pour their thundering streams into Acheron. When you reach this place, do as I tell you, my lord; dig a trench as long and as wide as a man's forearm. Go round this trench and pour offerings to all the dead, first with a mixture of honey and milk, then with sweet wine, and last of all with water. Over all this sprinkle white barley and then begin your prayers to the helpless ghosts of the dead. Promise them that once you are in Ithaca you will sacrifice a barren heifer in your palace, the best that you have, and will heap the pyre with treasures, and make Teiresias a separate offering of the finest jet-black sheep in your flock.

'"When you have finished your invocations to the glorious company of the dead, sacrifice a ram and a black ewe, holding their heads down towards Erebus while you turn your own aside, to face the River of Ocean. The spirits of the dead and departed will come up in their multitudes. Then you must immediately order your men to flay the sheep that are lying there slaughtered by your pitiless blade, and burn them sacrificially, praying to the gods, to mighty Hades and august Persephone. Sit still yourself meanwhile, with your drawn sword in your hand, and do not let any of the helpless ghosts come near to the blood till you have questioned Teiresias. Presently the prophet himself will come to you, my Lord King. And he will prophesy your route, the stages of your journey and how you will reach home across the teeming seas."

'Circe finished, and soon after, Dawn rose from her throne of gold. The Nymph dressed me in my tunic and cloak and herself put on a long robe of silvery sheen, of a light fabric charming to the eye. Round her waist she fastened a splendid golden belt, and she put a veil over her head. Then I walked through the palace and made the round of my men, rousing them each with a cheerful word. "Wake up," I said, "and bid your pleasant sleep farewell. It's time to go. My lady Circe has made everything clear."

'My gallant band agreed gladly enough. But even this time I did not lead them all safely away. There was one called Elpenor, the youngest of the party, not much of a fighting man and not very clever. This young man had got drunk, and longing for fresh air had left his friends and gone to sleep on the roof of Circe's enchanted palace. Roused in the morning by the bustle and the din of the departure, he leapt up suddenly, and forgetting to go to the long ladder and take the proper way down, he toppled headlong from the roof. He broke his neck and his soul went to Hades.

'When the rest of the party joined me I said to them: "You no doubt imagine that you are bound for home and our beloved Ithaca. But Circe has marked us out for a very different route – to the Halls of Hades and dread Persephone, where we must seek advice of the spirit of Theban Teiresias."

'When I told them this they were heart-broken. They sat down where they were and wept and tore their hair. But their lamentations achieved nothing.

'We made our way to our ship and the beach with heavy hearts and with many tears. Meanwhile Circe had gone ahead and tethered a ram and a black ewe by the ship. She had slipped past us with ease; when a god wishes to remain unseen, what eye can observe his coming or going?'

Scylla and Charybdis

'From the flowing waters of the River of Ocean my ship passed into the wide spaces of the open sea; and so reached the island of Aeaea, where, ever-fresh, Dawn has her home and her dancing-lawns, and where the Sun rises. Here we beached the ship on the sands and climbed out on to the shore, where we fell into a sound sleep, awaiting the coming of ethereal Dawn.

'As soon as she appeared, fresh and rosy-fingered, I sent off a party to Circe's house to fetch the dead body of Elpenor. We quickly chopped some logs, and then, with the tears streaming down our cheeks, performed the funeral rites on the summit of the boldest headland of the coast. When the corpse was burnt, and with it the dead man's armour, we built him a barrow, hauled up a stone for monument, and planted his shapely oar on the top of the mound.

'When we completed each of these rites, Circe became aware of our return from Hades, adorned herself, and came hurrying up with handmaidens laden with bread, a plentiful supply of meat and sparkling red wine.

'"What audacity," said the glorious goddess, as we gathered round her, "to descend alive into the House of Hades! Other men die once; you will now die twice. But come, spend the rest of the day here, enjoying this food and wine, and at daybreak tomorrow you shall sail. I myself will give you your route and make everything clear, to save you from the disasters you may suffer as a result of evil scheming on land or sea."

'We were not difficult to persuade. So the whole day long till sunset we sat and feasted on our rich supply of meat and mellow wine. When the sun sank and darkness fell, my men settled down for the night by the ships; but Circe took me by the hand, led me away from my good comrades, and made me sit down and tell her everything as she lay beside me. When I had given her the whole tale from first to last the Lady Circe said:

'"Very well; all that is done with now. But listen to my words – and some god will recall them to your mind. Your next encounter will be with the Sirens, who bewitch everybody who approaches them. There is no homecoming for the man who draws near them unawares and hears the Sirens' voices; no welcome from his wife, no little children brightening at their father's return. For with their high clear song the Sirens bewitch him, as they sit there in a meadow piled high with the mouldering skeletons of men, whose withered skin still hangs upon their bones. Drive your ship past the spot, and to prevent any of your crew from hearing, soften some beeswax and plug

41

their ears with it. But if you wish to listen yourself, make them bind you hand and foot on board and place you upright by the housing of the mast, with the rope's ends lashed to the mast itself. This will allow you to listen with enjoyment to the Sirens' voices. But if you beg and command your men to release you, they must add to the bonds that already hold you fast.

'"When your crew have carried you past the Sirens, two routes will be open to you. Though I cannot give you precise advice – you must choose for yourself – I will tell you about both. One leads to those sheer cliffs which the blessed gods know as the Wandering Rocks. Here blue-eyed Amphitrite sends her great breakers thundering in, and the very birds cannot fly by in safety, even the shy doves that bring ambrosia to Father Zeus; even of them the smooth rock always takes one, and the Father has to send one more to make their number up. For any sailors who bring their ship to the spot, there is no escape whatever. They end as flotsam on the sea, timbers and corpses tossed in confusion by the waves or licked up by tempestuous and destroying flames. Of all ships that go down to the sea one only has made the passage, and that was the celebrated *Argo*, homeward bound from Aeetes' coast. And the waves would soon have dashed her upon those mighty crags, if Hera, for love of Jason, had not helped her past.

'"In the other direction lie two rocks, one of which rears its sharp peak up to the very sky and is capped by black clouds that never stream away nor leave clear weather round the top, even in summer or at harvest-time. No man on earth could

42

climb to the top of it or even get a foothold on it, not even if he had twenty hands and feet to help him, because the rock is as smooth as if it had been polished. But half-way up the crag there is a murky cavern, facing the West and running down to Erebus, past which, illustrious Odysseus, you will probably steer your ship. Even a strong young bowman could not reach the gaping mouth of the cave with an arrow shot from a ship below.

"'It is the home of Scylla, the creature with the dreadful bark. It is true that her yelp is no louder than a new-born pup's, but she is a repulsive monster nevertheless. Nobody could look at her with delight, not even a god if he passed that way. She has twelve feet, all dangling in the air, and six long scrawny necks, each ending in a grisly head with triple rows of fangs, set thick and close, and darkly menacing death. Up to her waist she is sunk in the depths of the cave, but her heads protrude from the fearful abyss, and thus she fishes from her own abode, groping greedily around the rock for any dolphins or seals or any of the larger monsters which Amphitrite breeds in the roaring seas. No crew can boast that they ever sailed their ship past Scylla unscathed, for from every blue-prowed vessel she snatches and carries off a man with each of her heads.

"'The other of the two rocks, Odysseus, is lower, as you will see, and the distance between them is no more than a bowshot. A great fig-tree with luxuriant foliage grows upon the crag, and it is below this that dread Charybdis sucks the dark waters down. Three times a day she spews them up, and three times she swallows them down once more in her horrible

43

way. Heaven keep you from the spot when she does this because not even the Earthshaker could save you from destruction then. No, you must hug Scylla's rock and with all speed drive your ship through, since it is far better to lose six of your company than your whole crew."

"'Yes, goddess,' I replied, "but tell me this. I must be quite clear about it. Could I not somehow steer clear of the deadly Charybdis, yet ward off Scylla when she attacks my crew?"

"'Obstinate fool,' the beautiful goddess replied. "Again you are spoiling for a fight and looking for trouble! Are you not prepared to give in to immortal gods? I tell you, Scylla was not born for death: she is an undying fiend. She is a thing of terror, intractable, ferocious and impossible to fight. No, against her there is no defence, and the best course of action is flight. For if you waste time by the rock in putting on your armour, I am afraid she may dart out once more, make a grab with all six heads and snatch another six of your crew. So drive your ship past with all your might, and call on Cratais, Scylla's mother, who whelped her into the world to be the bane of mankind. She will prevent her from pouncing out again.

"'Next you will reach the island of Thrinacie, where many of the Sun-god's cattle and plump sheep graze. There are seven herds of cattle and as many flocks of beautiful sheep, with fifty head in each. No births increase or deaths decrease their numbers. And to shepherd them they have goddesses with braided hair, the Nymphs, Phaethusa and Lampetie, children of Hyperion the Sun-god by the resplendent Neaera, whom their mother, when she had brought them up, took away to this new and distant home in Thrinacie to watch over their father's sheep and crooked-horned cattle. Now if you leave them untouched and fix your mind on getting home, there is some chance that all of you may yet reach Ithaca, though not without suffering. But if you hurt them, then I predict the destruction of your ship and your company. And if you yourself contrive to escape, you will reach home late, in a wretched state, having lost all your comrades."

'As Circe came to an end, Dawn mounted her golden throne. The glorious goddess left me and made her way inland, while I went to my ship and ordered my men to embark and untie the hawsers. They did so promptly, went to the oars, sat down in their places and all together struck the grey surf with their blades. The Circe, that formidable goddess with the beautiful hair and a woman's voice, sent us the friendly escort of a favourable wind, which sprang up from astern and filled the sail of our blue-painted ship. We set the tackle in order fore and aft, then sat down, and the wind and the helmsman kept her on her course.

'Then, perturbed in spirit, I addressed my men. "My friends," I said, "it is not right that only one or two of us should know the prophecies that divine Circe has made to me, and I am going to pass them on to you, so that we may all be forewarned, whether we die, or escape the worst and save our lives. Her first warning concerned the Sirens with their divine song. We must beware of them and give their flowery meadow a wide berth, but she instructed me alone to hear their voices. You must bind me very tight, standing me up against the step of the mast and lashed to the mast itself so that I cannot stir from the spot. And if I beg and command you to release me, you must tighten and add to my bonds."

'In this way I explained every detail to my men. In the meantime our good ship, with that friendly breeze to drive her, fast approached the Sirens' isle. But now the wind dropped, some power lulled the waves, and a breathless calm set in. Rising from their seats my men drew in the sail and threw it into the hold, then sat down at the oars and churned the water white with their blades of polished pine. Meanwhile I took a large round of wax, cut it up with my sharp sword, and worked the pieces with all the strength of my fingers. The wax soon grew warm with my vigorous kneading and with the rays of the Sun-god, Hyperion's son. I took all my men in turn and plugged their ears with it. They then bound me hand and foot, standing me up by the step of the ship's mast and then lashing me to the mast itself. This done, they sat down once more and struck the grey water with their oars.

'We made good progress and had just come within call of the shore when the Sirens became aware that a ship was bearing down upon them, and broke into their high, clear song.

'"Draw near, illustrious Odysseus, man of many tales, great glory of the Achaeans, and bring your ship to rest so that you may hear our voices. No seaman ever sailed his black ship past this spot without listening to the honey-sweet tones that flow from our lips and no one who has listened has not been delighted and gone on his way a wiser man. For we know all that the Argives and Trojans suffered on the broad plain of Troy by the will of the gods, and we know whatever happens on this fruitful earth.''

'This was the sweet song the Sirens sang, and my heart was filled with such a longing to listen that I ordered my men to set me free, gesturing with my eyebrows. But they swung forward over their oars and rowed ahead, while Perimedes and Eurylochus jumped up, tightened my ropes and added more. However, when they had rowed past the Sirens and we could no longer hear the sound and the words of their song, my good companions were quick to clear their ears of the wax I had used to stop them, and to free me from the ropes that bound me.

'We had no sooner put this island behind us than I saw a cloud of spume ahead and a raging surf, and heard the thunder of the breakers. My men were so terrified that the oars all dropped from their grasp and fell with a splash on to the sea; and the ship herself, now that the hands that had pulled the smooth blades were idle, was brought to a standstill. I went up and down the ship, stood by each man and encouraged them with soothing words.

'"My friends," I said, "we are men who have met troubles before. And this trouble is no worse than when the Cyclops used his brutal strength to imprison us in his cave. Yet my courage, strategy and intelligence found a way out for us even from there; and I am sure that this too will be a memory for us one day. So now let us all agree to do exactly as I say. Oarsmen, stay at your oars, striking hard with your blades through the deep swell, in the hope that Zeus allows us to escape disaster and come out of this alive. Helmsman, your orders are these. Fix them in your mind, for the good ship's steering-oar is in your control. Give a wide berth to that foaming surf, and hug these cliffs, or before you can stop her the ship may take us over there and we'll be wrecked.''

'The crew obeyed me immediately. I did not mention the inescapable horror of Scylla, fearing that in their panic my men might stop rowing and huddle below the decks. But now I allowed myself to forget Circe's irksome instruction not to arm myself in any way. I put my famous armour on, seized a couple of long spears, and took my stand on the forecastle deck, hoping from there to get the first view of Scylla, the monster of the rocks, who was preparing disaster for my crew. But I could not catch a glimpse of her anywhere, though I searched the sombre face of the cliff in every part till my eyes were tired.

'Thus we sailed up the straits, wailing in terror, for on the one side we had Scylla, and on the other the awesome Charybdis sucked down the salt water in her dreadful way. When she vomited it up, she was stirred to her depths and seethed over like a cauldron on a blazing fire; and the spray she flung up rained down on the tops of the crags at either side. But when she swallowed the salt water down, the whole interior of her vortex was exposed, the rocks re-echoed to her fearful roar, and the dark blue sands of the sea-bed were exposed.

'My men turned pale with terror; and now, while all eyes were on Charybdis as the quarter from which we looked for disaster, Scylla snatched out of my ship the six strongest and ablest men. Glancing towards my ship, looking for my comrades, I saw their arms and legs dangling high in the air above my head. "Odysseus!" they called out to me in their anguish. But it was the last time they used my name. For like an angler on a jutting point, who casts his bait to lure the little fishes below, dangles his long rod with its line protected by an ox-horn pipe, gets a bite, and whips his struggling catch to land, Scylla had whisked my comrades, struggling, up the rocks. There she devoured them at her own door, shrieking and stretching out their hands to me in their last desperate throes. In all I have gone through as I explored the pathways of the seas, I have never had to witness a more pitiable sight than that.

'When we had left the Rocks, Scylla, and dreaded Charybdis behind, we soon reached the Sun-god's lovely isle, where Hyperion kept his splendid broad-browed cattle and his flocks of sturdy sheep. From where I was on board, out at sea, I could hear the lowing of cows as they were stalled for the night, and the bleating of sheep. And there came into my mind the words of Teiresias, the blind Theban prophet, and of Circe of Aeaea, who had each been so insistent in warning me to avoid this Island of the Sun, the comforter of mankind. So with an aching heart I addressed my men.

'"Comrades in suffering," I said, "listen to me while I tell you what Teiresias and Circe of Aeaea predicted. They warned me insistently to keep clear of the Island of the Sun, the comforter of mankind, for there, they said, our deadliest peril lurks. So drive the ship past the island."

'My men were heart-broken when they heard this, and Eurylochus spoke up at once in a hostile manner. "Odysseus, you are one of those hard men whose spirit never flags and whose body never tires. You must be made of iron through and through to forbid your men, worn out by our efforts and lack of sleep, to set foot on dry land, with the chance of cooking ourselves a tasty supper on this sea-girt isle. Instead, you expect us, just as we are, with night coming on fast, to abandon this island and go wandering off over the foggy sea. It is at night that high winds spring up and wreck ships. What port could we reach to save ourselves from going down if we were hit by a sudden squall from the south or the west? There's nothing like the South Wind or the wicked West for smashing a ship to pieces. And they don't ask leave of our lords the gods! No, let us give in to the evening dusk, and cook our supper by the side of the ship. In the morning we can go on board and put out into the open sea."

'This speech of Eurylochus was greeted by applause from all the rest, and it was brought home to me that some god really had a calamity in store for us. I answered him with words on wings: "Eurylochus, I am one against many, and you force my hand. Very well. But I call on every man of you to give his solemn promise that if we come across a herd of cattle or a large flock of sheep, he will not kill a single ox or sheep in a wanton fit of recklessness. Just sit peacefully and eat the food that the goddess Circe has provided."

'The crew agreed and gave the promise I had asked for. Accordingly, when all had sworn and completed the oath, we brought the good ship to anchor in a sheltered cove, with fresh water at hand, and the men disembarked and proceeded efficiently to prepare their supper. When they had satisfied their hunger and thirst, their thoughts returned to their dear comrades whom Scylla had snatched from the hollow ship and devoured; and they wept till soothing sleep overtook them.

'In the third watch of the night, when the stars had passed their zenith, Zeus the Cloud-gatherer whipped up a gale of incredible violence. He covered land and sea with clouds, and down sped night from heaven. As soon as Dawn came, fresh and rosy-fingered, we beached our ship and dragged her up into a hollow cave, which the Nymphs used as a dancing-ground and meeting-place. I ordered all my men to gather round, and gave them a warning. "My friends," I said, "since we have plenty of food and drink on board, let us keep our hands off these cattle, or we shall come to grief. For the cows and the fine sheep you have seen belong to that formidable god, the Sun, whose eyes and ears miss nothing."

'My strong-willed company accepted this. And now for a whole month the South Wind blew without a pause, and after that we had nothing but the South and the West winds. The men, so long as their bread and red wine lasted, kept their hands off the cattle as they valued their lives. But when the provisions in the ship gave out and the pangs of hunger sent them wandering with barbed hooks in quest of any game, fishes or birds, which might come to hand, I went inland to pray to the gods in the hope that one of them might show me a way of escape. When I had gone far enough across the island to be clear of the rest, I found a place that was sheltered from the wind, washed my hands, and made my supplications to the whole company of gods on Olympus.

They then cast me into a pleasant sleep. In the meantime Eurylochus was broaching a wicked scheme to his mates.

'"My comrades in suffering," he said, "listen to what I have to say. To us wretched men all forms of death are abominable, but death by starvation is the most miserable way to meet one's doom. So come, let us round up the best of the Sun's cows and sacrifice them in honour of the immortals who live in the broad sky. If ever we reach our homeland in Ithaca, our first act will be to build Hyperion the Sun-god a magnificent temple and fill it with precious offerings. But if in anger at the loss of his straight-horned herds he chooses to wreck our ship, with the support of the other gods, I would sooner drown instantly in a watery grave than waste away by slow degrees on a desert island."

'His ideas found favour with the rest, and they proceeded at once to round up the pick of the Sun-god's cattle. They had not far to go, for the fine cows with their broad foreheads and twisted horns used to graze in the neighbourhood of our blue-prowed ship. The men gathered round the cattle and made their prayers to the gods, using for the ceremony some fresh leaves they stripped from a tall oak-tree, since they had no white barley on the ship. Their prayers done, they slit the cows' throats and flayed them, then cut out slices from the thighs, wrapped them in folds of fat and laid raw meat above them. And since they had no wine to pour over the burning sacrifice, they made libations with water as they roasted all the entrails. When the thighs were burnt up and they had tasted the inner parts, they carved the rest into small pieces and spitted them on skewers.

'Then it was that I suddenly awoke from my deep sleep, and started on my way back to the vessel and the coast. Directly I came near my curved ship the sweet smell of roasting meat wafted all about me. I exclaimed in horror and called out to the immortal gods. "Father Zeus and you other blessed gods who live for ever! So it was to ruin me that you lulled me into that cruel sleep, while left to themselves my men planned this awful crime!"

'A swift messenger, Lampetie herself, Lampetie of the trailing robes, ran to the Sun-god Hyperion with news that we had killed his cattle; and in a fury he cried out to the immortals: "Father Zeus and you other blessed gods who live for ever, take vengeance on the followers of Odysseus son of Laertes. They have criminally killed my cattle, the cattle that gave me such joy every day as I climbed the starry sky and as I dropped down from heaven and sank once more to earth. If they do not repay me in full for my slaughtered cows, I will go down to the realm of Hades and shine among the dead."

'"Sun," the Cloud-gatherer answered him, "shine on for the immortals and for mortal men on the fruitful earth. As for the culprits, I will soon strike their ship with a blinding bolt out on the wine-dark sea and smash it to pieces."

'This part of the tale I had from Calypso of the beautiful hair, who told me that she herself had heard it from Hermes the Messenger.

'When I had come down to the sea and reached the ship, I confronted my men one after the other and rebuked them. But we could find no way of mending matters: the cows were dead. And the gods soon began to show my crew ominous portents.

The hides began to crawl about; the meat, roast and raw, bellowed on the spits; and a sound as of lowing cattle could be heard.

'For six days my men feasted on the pick of the Sun's cattle they had rounded up. But when Zeus brought the seventh day, the fury of the gale abated, and we quickly embarked and put out into the open sea after stepping the mast and hauling up the white sail.

'When we had left the island astern and no other land or anything but sky and water, was to be seen, Zeus brought a sombre cloud to rest above the hollow ship so that the sea was darkened by its shadow. Before she had run very far, a howling wind suddenly sprang up from the west and hit us with hurricane force. The squall snapped both forestays simultaneously. As the mast toppled, all the rigging tumbled into the hold, and the mast itself, reaching the stern, struck the helmsman on the head and smashed in all the bones of his skull. He plunged like a diver from the deck, and his brave soul left his body. Then at one and the same moment Zeus thundered and struck the vessel with lightning. The whole ship reeled from the blow of his bolt and was filled with the smell of sulphur. My men were flung overboard and round the black hull they floated like sea-gulls on the waves. There was no homecoming for them: the god saw to that.

'Meanwhile I kept shifting from one part of the ship to another, till a great wave tore her sides from her keel, which the sea then swept along denuded of its ribs. It snapped the mast off close to the keel, but as the backstay, which was a leather rope, had fallen across the mast, I used it to lash mast and keel together, and astride these two timbers I became the sport of the furious winds.

'The storm that had blown up from the west subsided soon enough, but was quickly followed by more wind from the south, to my great distress, for this meant that I should have once more to retrace my course to the dread Charybdis. All through the night I was swept along, and at sunrise found myself back at Scylla's rock and that appalling whirlpool. Charybdis was beginning to suck the salt water down. But as she did so, I swung myself up to the great fig-tree, on which I got a tight grip and clung like a bat. I could find no foothold to support me, or any means of climbing into the tree, for its roots were far away below, and the great long branches that overshadowed Charybdis stretched high above my head.

'However, I clung grimly on until she spewed up my mast and keel once more. I longed for them to reappear, and in the end they did, at the time of day when a judge with a long list of disputes to settle between obstinate litigants rises from court for his evening meal. Then at last the timbers reappeared on the surface. I let go, and dropped with sprawling hands and feet, to splash into the water clear of the great logs. I clambered on to them, and paddled along with my hands. And thanks to the Father of men and Gods Scylla did not catch sight of me. Otherwise nothing could have saved me from certain death.

'Nine days of drifting followed; but in the night of the tenth the gods washed me up on the island of Ogygia, the home of Calypso of the braided tresses, that formidable goddess with a woman's voice; and she received me kindly and looked after me. But why go again through all this? Only yesterday I told you and your noble wife the whole story here in your home, and it is tedious for me to repeat a tale already plainly told.'

READ MORE IN PENGUIN

For complete information about books available from Penguin and how to order them, please write to us at the appropriate address below. Please note that for copyright reasons the selection of books varies from country to country.

IN THE UNITED KINGDOM: Please write to *Dept. EP, Penguin Books Ltd, Bath Road, Harmondsworth, Middlesex UB7 0DA.*

IN THE UNITED STATES: Please write to *Consumer Sales, Penguin USA, P.O. Box 999, Dept. 17109, Bergenfield, New Jersey 07621-0120.* VISA and MasterCard holders call 1-800-253-6476 to order Penguin titles.

IN CANADA: Please write to *Penguin Books Canada Ltd, 10 Alcorn Avenue, Suite 300, Toronto, Ontario M4V 3B2.*

IN AUSTRALIA: Please write to *Penguin Books Australia Ltd, P.O. Box 257, Ringwood, Victoria 3134.*

IN NEW ZEALAND: Please write to *Penguin Books (NZ) Ltd, Private Bag 102902, North Shore Mail Centre, Auckland 10.*

IN INDIA: Please write to *Penguin Books India Pvt Ltd, 706 Eros Apartments, 56 Nehru Place, New Delhi 110 019.*

IN THE NETHERLANDS: Please write to *Penguin Books Netherlands bv, Postbus 3507, NL-1001 AH Amsterdam.*

IN GERMANY: Please write to *Penguin Books Deutschland GmbH, Metzlerstrasse 26, 60594 Frankfurt am Main.*

IN SPAIN: Please write to *Penguin Books S. A., Bravo Murillo 19, 1º B, 28015 Madrid.*

IN ITALY: Please write to *Penguin Italia s.r.l., Via Felice Casati 20, I–20124 Milano.*

IN FRANCE: Please write to *Penguin France S. A., 17 rue Lejeune, F–31000 Toulouse.*

IN JAPAN: Please write to *Penguin Books Japan, Ishikiribashi Building, 2–5–4, Suido, Bunkyo-ku, Tokyo 112.*

IN GREECE: Please write to *Penguin Hellas Ltd, Dimocritou 3, GR–106 71 Athens.*

IN SOUTH AFRICA: Please write to *Longman Penguin Southern Africa (Pty) Ltd, Private Bag X08, Bertsham 2013.*